Raintree is an imprint of Capstone Global Library Limited, a company
incorporated in England and Wales having its registered office at 264 Banbury
Road, Oxford, OX2 7DY – Registered company number: 6695582

www.raintree.co.uk
myorders@raintree.co.uk

Designed by Hilary Wacholz
Original illustrations © Capstone Global Library Limited 2019
Originated by Capstone Global Library Ltd
Printed and bound in India

ISBN 978 1 4747 6200 7
22 21 20 19 18
10 9 8 7 6 5 4 3 2 1

British Library Cataloguing in Publication Data
A full catalogue record for this book is available from the British Library.

The Funny Girl

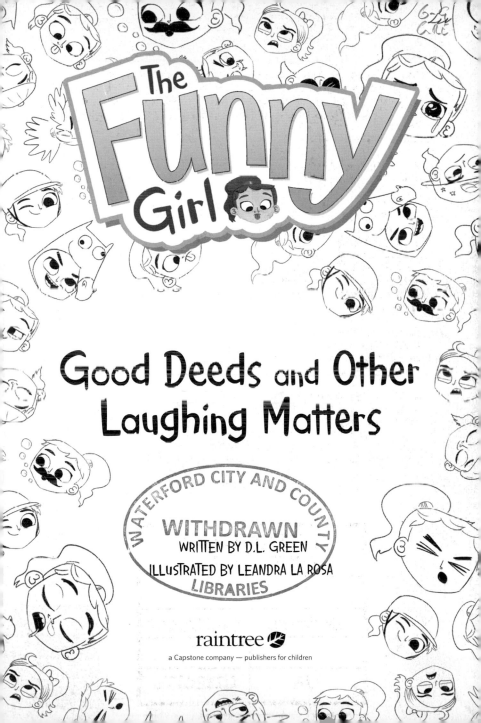

Good Deeds and Other Laughing Matters

WRITTEN BY D.L. GREEN

ILLUSTRATED BY LEANDRA LA ROSA

raintree 🍃

a Capstone company — publishers for children

CONTENTS

GOODBYE, WORLD. NICE KNOWING YOU.

I did not like Brooke Crumpkin. She did not like me. I did not like the things Brooke liked. Brooke did not like the things I liked.

Brooke and I had exactly four things in common. We were both girls, we went to the same school, we were both in the same year and we had the same teacher. But we never agreed on anything.

These are the things Brooke liked most in the world:

1. Brooke
2. Fashion
3. Being mean to people

I did not like any of those things. I especially did not like number one on the list.

These are the things I liked most:

1. Jokes
2. Horses
3. My dog, Mugsy

Brooke did not like any of those things.

Well, she had never met Mugsy, but once I heard her say dogs were gross.

Mugsy was huge and shed his hair all over the place. He loved to sniff other dogs' poo. Sometimes he drooled. But I did not think he was gross at all.

Before school started one morning, Brooke and some other kids and I stood in the corridor outside our classroom. Brooke said, "I want to buy a Marvellous Gizmo."

I nodded in amazement.

For the first time ever, Brooke Crumpkin and I agreed about something. I wanted to buy a Marvellous Gizmo too. I wanted a Marvellous Gizmo more than anything. In fact, I should have added Marvellous Gizmos to the list of things I liked most. If I had to choose only three things I liked most, I might even have knocked my dog off the list. His drooling *was* kind of gross. (Sorry, Mugsy.)

I didn't know what exactly Marvellous Gizmos *did*, but I was dying to have one. I had seen about a thousand ads for them on TV and online. They all said Marvellous Gizmos were the coolest things ever. So they had to be great. Plus they cost a lot of money. Anything that cost a lot of money had to be great.

Brooke was talking and talking. "I'm going to have the best Marvellous Gizmo of anyone. I'll bring it to school. But I won't let anyone touch it or even look at—"

"That's rude," I said.

"Interrupting me is rude," Brooke said. She stamped her foot. It landed on a piece of scrunched-up chocolate bar wrapper someone had left behind. The wrapper had a big brown smudge on it.

"Disgusting!" she said.

For the second time *ever*, I agreed with Brooke. Litter really was disgusting. There was a lot of litter in the corridor. It looked like someone had spilled a backpack full of paper and wrappers – someone who really liked chocolate bars.

"Someone should do something about this litter," Brooke said.

I nodded. I also wished someone would do something about the litter.

That meant Brooke Crumpkin and I had agreed about three things in one morning. Had the world gone mad? Had Earth spun off its axis?

"I'm tired of standing here," Brooke said. "I wish Ms Fish would hurry and let us in."

"Me too," I said. Then I clamped my hand over my mouth. Brooke and I had just agreed on a fourth thing. Was the world about to explode?

BROOKE AND SHELBY SAVE THE WORLD

A few minutes later, our teacher, Ms Fish, arrived and opened the classroom door. She smiled and said, "Good morn—"

"It's about time," Brooke interrupted her. She shoved past some kids near the door and barged into the classroom. Other kids shoved their way inside too.

"No 'sorry' or 'excuse me'?" the teacher asked.

"You're forgiven and excused," I joked. I was the new kid in class, so I had to be funny.

"Good one," said Ajay Patel.

Ajay was my friend and neighbour, and he almost always liked my jokes.

Right before the bell rang, another new friend, Gabby Garcia, ran into the classroom. She said, "Sorry, Ms Fish. I picked up the litter outside our classroom and threw it away. It almost made me late."

"Thank you for doing that, Gabby," Ms Fish said. "The rest of you disappointed me this morning. You walked right through that mess and left it there. You pushed and shoved each other. You interrupted me. And you did not say good morning."

"What did we do wrong?" I joked.

The class laughed.

Ms Fish frowned and said, "I have decided to do something about your poor behaviour."

Uh-oh. Was Ms Fish going to keep us inside for break time? Give us extra homework? Make us stay after school? Whatever it was, I wanted no part of it.

"I'm going to give out an award," Ms Fish said.

An award? *That* I wanted a part of. I wanted a big part of that. In fact, I wanted the whole thing.

"The nicest, politest and most helpful pupil in the class will win the Good Person Award," Ms Fish said.

"What do we get for the Good Person Award?" Brooke asked.

Ms Fish gave Brooke a pointed look. "A good person puts her hand up in class."

Brooke put up her hand. Before Ms Fish could call on her, she repeated, "What do we get for the Good Person Award?"

"Let's just say that winning the award will be worth your while," Ms Fish said.

I put up my hand and asked, "Is it money?"

Ms Fish smiled and repeated, "It'll be worth your while."

Ooh, that must mean money. What's more worth your while than money? I thought. Then I realized I could use the award money to buy a Marvellous Gizmo. I decided right then that I needed to win the award.

"I am going to win the award," Brooke announced.

"You forgot to put up your hand again," I said. **"The odds of you winning the Good Person Award are about as good as an elephant winning a game of hide-and-seek."**

"Shelby, you *look* like an elephant," Brooke replied.

"Girls, you are both behaving badly," Ms Fish said, shaking her head.

Ms Fish was right. We wouldn't win the Good Person Award by insulting each other.

"I'm sorry," I said. "A good person apologizes."

"I'm even more sorry." Brooke glared at me. "And I'm even more good."

I glared at Brooke. "I'm the sorriest of all."

"You're wrong," Brooke said. Then she added, "A good person compliments people. Ms Fish, I like your top."

"Ms Fish, I like your top *and* your trousers," I said.

"Shelby, you don't know anything about fashion," Brooke said.

"Brooke, you don't know anything about being a good person," I said.

Just then I realized something: Brooke and I were disagreeing again. The world wasn't going mad, spinning off its axis or exploding. I sighed with relief.

Then I smiled as I thought about winning the Good Person Award. As soon as I got the award money, I'd hurry to the toy shop and buy a Marvellous Gizmo. I'd take it to school, play with it right in front of Brooke and tell her not to touch it.

This was great! To make Brooke feel bad, all I had to do was be a good person.

HOW TO BE A GOOD PERSON

Being at school all day hurt my brain. After school I usually gave my brain a nice, long rest. But not that day. I needed to keep my brain whirling and buzzing, planning how to win the Good Person Award.

It was going to be a challenge. I knew I was nice, polite and helpful. But to win the award, I would have to be nicer, politer and more helpful than anyone in my class.

As I headed to the school bus with Gabby, I tried to think of ways I could do that. While I walked, I kicked a lunch box that someone had left on the playground.

"I'll take this to Lost and Found," Gabby said, picking up the lunch box and interrupting my thoughts.

"Shhh," I said. "I'm trying to think of ways to win the Good Person Award."

But Gabby kept talking. "Do you want to come with me?"

I shook my head. "I'm too busy thinking about how to be nice, polite and helpful."

"I help out at the school library a couple of days a week after school," Gabby said. "I put books back on the shelves and—"

"You're interrupting my thoughts about the award," I said. "It's rude."

"I was just trying to—"

"You're interrupting my thoughts again," I said.

"Sorry," Gabby said, looking a little hurt. "Well, I'll see you tomor—"

"Goodbye," I said.

I got in the queue for my bus and took a bag of crisps out of my backpack. I needed brain food. *Potatoes must be brain food*, I thought.

Ajay queued up behind me. He carried a big backpack, a bulky poster board for a science project, a basketball and a thin jacket.

"Could you please carry my jacket for me?" he asked.

"Sorry, but my hands are full." I held up a small bag of crisps. Then I climbed the steps and took a seat.

It took Ajay a long time to get on the bus because he was holding so much stuff. Finally he sat next to me. My older sister, Miss Priss, sat behind us. Her real name is Lila. I call her Miss Priss for two reasons:

1. She acts prissy.

2. She does not like to be called Miss Priss.

I turned to Ajay and said, "I've worked out how to win the Good Person Award. I'll keep telling jokes so I can

become a rich and famous comedian. Then I'll donate a thousand dollars to charity."

"Becoming rich and famous takes a long time," Ajay said. "I doubt you'll be rich *or* famous before Ms Fish gives out the Good Person Award."

"Oh." I slumped in my seat. "You're probably right."

Then I sat up and said, "How about this plan? I'll stow away on a fire engine. When we get to a fire, I'll jump out, run into the burning building and carry people out of it."

Ajay shook his head. "You just told me you couldn't carry my jacket. How are you going to carry a person out of a burning building?"

"Oh." I slumped in my seat again.

Then I got another great idea. I sat up again and said, "Instead of rescuing a person from a burning building, I'll rescue a pet. It will have to be a small pet that I can carry. But not a lizard or snake or any reptile. I don't like reptiles. And no cats. I don't want to get scratched. Maybe a rabbit."

"Rabbits can bite," Ajay said.

I sighed. "Forget it."

"Shelby, you don't sound like a good person to me," Lila piped up behind me.

"You sound like Miss Priss to me," I said.

I slumped in my seat again. Who knew being a good person was so hard?

ITCHING FOR A MARVELLOUS GIZMO

I stared sadly out of the bus window as we bounced along a busy street. I was about to give up on trying to win the Good Person Award. I would have to find another way to get some money.

Suddenly, my sadness disappeared. "I see a sign!" I squealed. "I have to win the award!"

"A sign that you should be a good person?" Ajay asked.

"What kind of sign? A lightning bolt? A cloud shaped like an angel?"

"No. That sign." I pointed at a huge billboard that said, "Marvellous Gizmos: The coolest toy ever."

I said, "I need to win the Good Person Award so I can buy a Marvellous Gizmo."

Ajay pressed his face against the window. Then he looked at me and rolled his eyes.

When I got home, my four-year-old brother, Coop, ran to the door. He said, "Hi, Shelby. Do you want to see what I made at preschool today? It took me a long—"

"I don't have time," I said. "I have to think about being a good person." I hurried past him and went to my bedroom to think in peace.

But Miss Priss had got there first. It wasn't just *my* bedroom. I had to share it with my sister. I did not like sharing a bedroom. I *really* did not like sharing a bedroom with her.

Miss Priss was sitting on her bed, kissing a picture of

her favourite singer, Dalton Dash. I also really did not like Dalton Dash. And I really, really did not like kissing.

Lila looked up from the picture and said, "Shelby, you've got dirty clothes all over the floor."

"Yes, I have," I said. Then I took off my jumper and threw it on the carpet.

"You don't sound like a good person to me," Lila said.

I stuck out my tongue at her.

Then I lay on my bed and thought about how to be a good person. I thought and thought about it for two hours. (Well, one hour and fifty-seven minutes of that time was spent napping.) But I still couldn't work out how to win the Good Person Award.

I went into the kitchen for a snack. My mum and dad were there, making dinner.

"Do you know how I can be a good person?" I asked them.

"There's a lot to do in the kitchen," Dad said as he peeled a carrot.

"Delicious food doesn't cook itself," Mum said as she grated cheese.

Dad started singing, "We all pitch in! In the kitchen!"

I did not want to pitch in. And I really did not want to hear Dad sing.

But he kept going: "I bet you're itching! For chopping and mixing!"

"Thanks, Mum and Dad," I said. "Now I know how to be a good person."

"Thank *you*, Shelby." Mum held up the block of cheese.

I slowly backed away. "Once you've finished making dinner and washing up, I'll bake brownies for my class."

THE THOUSAND-HOUR BROWNIES

Making brownies was extremely hard work. I had to:

1. Ask my dad for a recipe for brownies.

2. Ask my dad where we kept the vanilla, flour, baking powder, chocolate chips and cocoa powder.

3. Ask my dad to take the flour and baking powder down from the top shelf.

4. Ask my dad to go to the shop to buy chocolate chips and cocoa powder.

5. Put all the ingredients on the kitchen worktop.

6. Mix the ingredients together.

7. Ask my dad to help with the mixing.

8. Ask my dad to turn on the oven.

9. Ask my dad to put the brownies in the oven.

10. Wait for the brownies to bake.

While the brownies baked, I watched my favourite TV series, *Gotcha*. The Gotcha Gang had taped a guy's door shut, trapping him inside. I laughed so hard!

"That Gotcha Gang is mean," Lila said.

"Don't be prissy," I said. "They're funny."

Lila wrinkled her nose. "What's that bad smell?"

I pointed at her. "The smell of a rotten sister."

"You don't sound like a good person to me," Lila said.

Before I could respond, an advert came on for Marvellous Gizmos, the coolest toys ever. Lila and I stared silently at the TV.

After the advert ended, Lila said, "Really, what's that bad smell?"

"Your breath," I joked.

Lila sniffed the air. "Something's burning."

"The brownies!" I shouted. I ran into the kitchen.

Mum ran in after me. She took the brownies out of the oven and said, "You burned them."

"*I* didn't burn them," I said. "The *oven* burned them."

Lila walked into the kitchen. She said, "Shelby, you're the one who let the brownies burn."

"No one asked you, Miss Priss," I said.

"Now you're calling me names," Lila said. "You really don't sound like a good person to me."

I walked out of the kitchen so I could watch TV.

"Shelby Olivia Bloom," Mum called after me.

I was pretty sure Mum was mad, because:

1. She had called me by my full name.

2. Her voice was a lot louder than normal.

"Come back here," Mum added.

I went back there. Mum was definitely mad, because:

1. Her face was red.

2. She was frowning.

"You've made a giant mess in the kitchen," Mum said.

"It looks like a small mess to me," I said.

"Good," Mum said. "Then it shouldn't take you long to clean it up."

I let out a big sigh.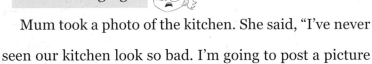

Mum took a photo of the kitchen. She said, "I've never seen our kitchen look so bad. I'm going to post a picture of it on my blog."

Why would people want to see a picture of a messy kitchen? I had no idea. Mum was always taking photos and posting them on her blog. Her blog was called Mum-O-Rama, and it had become a big hit. Thousands of people read it every day.

It took me about a thousand hours to clean the kitchen. Then Mum said it still looked messy. So I had to wipe the batter off the worktop, sweep the flour from

the floor, wash the mixing bowl with soap and hot water, and do a thousand other things.

"Look on the bright side," Mum said. "The picture of our messy kitchen got a lot of LOLs and likes on my blog."

I scowled. "I don't see anything bright about working so hard and being laughed at just so I can make burnt brownies."

I wondered if Ms Fish would find anything bright about it. By *bright*, I meant worthy of the Good Person Award.

A CRUMB-Y MORNING

Taking brownies to my class was hard work. Before I even left for school the next morning, I had to:

1. Ask my dad to cut the brownies into squares.

2. Ask my dad to cover the brownies with foil.

3. Tell my dad that I couldn't cover the brownies myself because I had homework due today.

4. Listen to my dad lecture about doing homework on time.

5. Listen to my mum lecture about doing homework on time.

6. Listen to Lila say, "You don't sound like a good person to me."

7. Ask my mum for a lift to the bus stop.

8. Tell my mum that I couldn't walk to the bus stop because I didn't want to drop the brownies. Also, it was a bit chilly outside.

After Mum drove me to the bus stop, I sat on the bus with the brownies on my lap. As soon as we pulled up to my school, I rushed off and hurried to my classroom. Ms Fish was the only person there. She sat at her desk, marking our maths tests.

I started putting a brownie on each kid's desk.

Ms Fish said, "Shelby, what are you doing?"

"Passing out my homemade brownies," I said. "Because I'm a good person."

"Did you wash your hands?" Ms Fish asked.

I nodded. I had washed my hands, though I couldn't remember exactly when. I was pretty sure I had washed my hands yesterday.

Other kids started walking into the room. I told them, "I made brownies for everyone because I'm a good person."

"Thanks. I was starving," Latasha Kennedy said.

It felt kind of good to help out.

"Did you bring plates or napkins?" Ms Fish asked.

Oops. I hadn't thought about that. I said, "I'm sure everyone can eat the brownies nice and neatly. We all have good manners."

Nick Sparangus let out a loud burp.

Latasha said, "The bottom of my brownie was burned. I left the burned crumbs on my desk."

"I dropped my burned crumbs on the floor," Tessa Lee said.

Ms Fish shook her head. "Crumbs should go in the bin."

Brooke put up her hand and said, "Crumbs from Shelby's burned brownies are all over the desks and floor. I don't think she should win the Good Person Award."

"Be quiet," I said. "I'm a very good person."

"Stop arguing," Ms Fish said. "Everyone take out your maths books."

"But we're still eating our brownies," I said.

Demi Wilson put up her hand. "I can't eat the brownies. I'm allergic to chocolate."

Jessica Cho put up her hand. "I'm allergic to eggs."

Jack Lopez didn't bother to put up his hand. He shouted, "I'm gluten free!"

Will Carelli said, "I'm allergic to chocolate *and* eggs. Plus I'm gluten free and vegan."

"Everyone settle down and focus on maths," Ms Fish said.

"Thank you for bringing in the brownies, Shelby," Gabby said. "You are thoughtful and nice."

"And a good person, right?" I asked.

Gabby nodded.

"The most good person in the class?" I asked.

I couldn't tell whether Gabby nodded again. She was too busy crawling on the floor, cleaning up everyone's brownie crumbs.

ALLERGIC TO BROOKE

At lunchtime I sat with my friends Alice and Rose. Alice wore a T-shirt that said, "Marvellous Gizmos: The coolest toys ever!"

"Did you get a Marvellous Gizmo?" I asked.

Alice frowned and shook her head. "My mum said they cost too much money. She got me this T-shirt instead."

"It's a nice T-shirt," I said. "But the toy is a lot cooler."

"It's the coolest toy ever," Alice and I said at the same time.

"What is a Marvellous Gizmo anyway?" Rose asked.

"The coolest toy ever," Alice and I said again.

"But what *is* it?" Rose asked.

"The coolest toy ever," Alice and I repeated.

Rose shrugged and bit into her sandwich.

I might not know the specifics now, but after I won the Good Person Award and bought a Marvellous Gizmo, I'd find out exactly what it was. I knew it would be great.

As I walked into my classroom after lunch, I saw Brooke's parents there. If her parents had been called into school, Brooke must have done something terrible. I smiled. Brooke would never get the Good Person Award now!

Brooke's mother opened a large pink box and pulled out a tall, fancy cake. She said, "Brooke asked us to buy a cake for the class. This has three layers: white cake, chocolate and strawberry. There's also buttercream

filling, chocolate fudge frosting, whipped cream and cherries."

"My cake is much better than Shelby's burned brownies," Brooke said.

"You didn't make the cake," I said. "Your parents bought it."

"So?" Brooke said.

"So you don't deserve the Good Person Award," I said.

Brooke scowled at me.

Brooke's dad opened a large white box. He took out red cloth napkins, china plates and gold forks.

"Shelby didn't bring any plates and napkins, but I brought all this," Brooke said. "I am such a good person."

I glared at Brooke and said, "Your *parents* brought all this."

"I'm allergic to this cake too," Will Carelli said.

"Me too," Demi Wilson said.

Jessica Cho put up her hand. "I bet this cake has eggs in it. I'm allergic to eggs."

Jack Lopez said, "This cake does not look vegan or gluten-free. I can't eat it."

Gabby put up her hand and said, "I felt bad for the kids who have allergies. So I bought vegan, gluten-free cupcakes with no chocolate or eggs in them." She gave everyone a cupcake and a napkin.

"You girls have been very thoughtful," Ms Fish said. "But we haven't spent much time learning today."

"We learned a lot about allergies today," Ajay said.

"And yesterday you told the class that learning long division was a piece of cake," I said to Ms Fish. "So all those pieces of cake mean we learned a lot of long division."

The class laughed.

"I learned that if I eat a brownie, a piece of cake and a cupcake, my stomach will hurt," Darla Jones said. Then she threw up in the bin.

"Oh no!" Ms Fish said.

"The smell of vomit makes me sick," Will Carelli said. Then he threw up in his lunch box.

Everyone moved away from Darla and Will and the vomit. Brooke's parents hurried out of the classroom.

"I'm making a new rule," Ms Fish said. "No one is allowed to bring in class treats anymore."

Brooke groaned and said, "Shelby ruined things for everyone."

"*You* ruined things for everyone," I said. But I knew we both had. I also knew that bringing brownies to class would not help me earn the Good Person Award.

D IS FOR
DISASTER

After school the next day, Gabby and I headed for the school library. Gabby had been shelving books there twice a week for a long time. I needed to do *something* good, so I was going to shelve books too.

As we walked, I said, "I think shelving books will make me as bored as a piece of wood."

Gabby laughed. "I get it. Bored as a board."

"Bored as a bored board in a boardroom," I said.

"You don't *have* to shelve books," Gabby said.

"Yes, I do. I need to prove I'm a good person." I sighed. "Taking in brownies yesterday didn't work out very well."

"Ms Fish definitely wasn't happy about all the ants in the classroom this morning," Gabby said.

"You should have done a better job of getting the brownie crumbs off the floor," I said.

Gabby raised her eyebrows.

"I guess I could have helped you," I admitted. "I'm the one who brought in the brownies."

"There were cake and cupcake crumbs on the floor too," Gabby said as she held open the library door for me.

As I looked at the thousands of books around us, I asked Gabby, "Why do you shelve books twice a week? Does the librarian pay you?"

Gabby shook her head. "I get paid in gratitude."

"Gratitude? Is that like getting paid in nickels or pesos or bitcoins?" I asked.

"Not really." Gabby shrugged. "It just makes me happy to help people."

Gabby really was strange. I didn't tell her that because I was a good person.

There were only a few other kids in the library when we got there. Each of them sat alone at a table.

The librarian wore bright red lipstick and earrings with long feathers on them. She waved at us and said, "Here comes my favourite pupil."

"Thank you," I joked.

"I meant Gabby," she said.

"Well, you're my favourite librarian," I said. "My favourite *school* librarian, at least. I like the one at the county library near my house. I also liked the librarian at my old school. OK, you're my favourite librarian *at this school*."

"I'm the *only* librarian at this school," she said.

"That means you're the very best, number one librarian at this school," I said. "Congratulations."

She laughed.

"Ms Spindler, this is my friend Shelby Bloom," Gabby told the librarian. "Shelby wants to help me shelve books every week."

I shook my head. "I'm just helping out today, for one hour, really. I never said I'd shelve books every week."

"You don't have to help out every week," Gabby said.

"Good. I have other important things to do with my time," I said. For instance, I needed time to watch TV.

"Are you ready to shelve books?" Ms Spindler asked.

I was not ready to be bored as a board. So I said, "Do you have any joke books? After I look through them, I might have some time to shelve books."

"Shelve the books first." Ms Spindler pointed to a trolley filled with about a thousand picture books. She said, "The preschool kids were here this morning and made a mess."

I frowned. "Ugh. Baby books."

"We're happy to help you," Gabby said to the librarian.

We wheeled the trolley over to the little kids' section of the library. Gabby and I carried a large stack of books from the trolley to a nearby table. She said, "Let's arrange the books in alphabetical order before we put them on the shelf."

"Good plan," I said. It felt kind of good to help out.

As I moved books from the trolley to the table, I said, "Do you know there are only eleven letters in the alphabet?"

Gabby glanced at me. "Huh?"

I spelled out, "T-H-E A-L-P-H-A-B-E-T. Eleven letters."

Gabby laughed.

"Yesterday I caught my dog eating a book," I said.

"Really?" Gabby asked as she sorted the books.

"I had to take the words right out of his mouth," I said.

Gabby laughed again. Then she said, "What do librarians take on fishing trips?"

"What?" I asked.

"Bookworms."

I laughed.

Gabby pointed to a pile of books and said, "I alphabetized these. Please help me get them onto the shelves."

Gabby was so bossy. She wouldn't win the Good Person Award.

I looked at the table. There were three tall stacks of books on it. I picked up the top book from one of the stacks and said, "I remember this book: *Put Me in the Zoo.*"

"Ms Spindler will put *you* in the zoo if you don't start shelving," Gabby said.

I laughed and flipped through the book as Gabby carried some of the sorted books to the shelf.

"Gabby, look at this funny picture," I said.

She put some books on the top shelf. It was rude of her to ignore me. She would never win the Good Person Award.

I spotted another great book. "Ooh, *Knuffle Bunny!*" I said. "I used to love this one! Mo Willems is the greatest."

I tried to slide the book from the bottom of one of the tall piles.

Worst mistake ever. All of the books from the top half of the pile fell over. They tumbled into the pile next to them. That pile tumbled into the pile next to it. Then everything fell down, like dominos – like the loudest, most ruinous, most awful game of dominos ever. Except it wasn't a game.

IT'S HARD WORK TO WATCH PEOPLE WORK

Everything seemed to go into slow motion, as the books crashed to the floor in loud cracks and claps. It was a disaster.

The librarian ran over to Gabby and me and the books on the floor. All the kids who had been sitting by themselves came running too.

"Is everything OK?" Ms Spindler asked.

"Don't worry," I said. "No one got hurt."

"I was asking if everything was OK with my books," Ms Spindler said.

Gabby started putting the books back on the table.

I held up a copy of *Go, Dog, Go.* "I suppose the dogs really wanted to go – right onto the floor."

Gabby and the other kids laughed.

Then I picked up *The Runaway Bunny.* "The bunny really did run away. He ran from the table and landed on the floor."

They laughed some more.

I picked up *Don't Let the Pigeon Drive the Bus.* "Don't let the pigeon drive the bus and don't let kids shelve the books."

The kids laughed again.

One of the boys said to the boy next to him, "That girl is funny."

Ms Spindler crossed her arms. "I don't find anything funny about my books falling all over the floor and getting bashed."

"I'll pick up the books and shelve them," Gabby said.

Ms Spindler frowned. "It will take you a long time. The library closes in an hour."

"If all the kids here pitched in and shelved the books, it wouldn't take that long," I said.

The other kids all offered to help. We quickly picked up the books and put them on the table. Gabby and two older kids alphabetized the books. Two younger boys put them on the shelves. I sat on a chair, leafed through some books, and watched the other kids work. That made me feel guilty. So I stopped watching them.

"I feel sorry for maths books," I said.

"Why?" one of the boys asked.

"Because they have a lot of problems," I said.

Everyone laughed.

Then I said, "Why was the dinosaur afraid to go to the library?"

"Why?" Gabby asked.

"Because his books were ten million years overdue."

Everyone laughed again.

Gabby and the other kids finished shelving the books.

The librarian came by and said, "Thank you, everyone, for your hard work." Then she looked at me and said, "Well, *almost* everyone."

"I did my part," I said.

Ms Spindler crossed her arms. "Your part involved knocking over books, sitting around and telling jokes."

"It was Shelby's idea to get everyone to help," one of the older kids said.

"That's right," Gabby said. "Shelby also entertained everyone. She made it fun to shelve books. Shelby's a good person."

Ms Spindler kept her arms crossed.

I knew I would not be shelving library books again. I hoped I would not get banned from ever entering the library again. And I really hoped the librarian wouldn't tell Ms Fish what I had done today.

TRIPLE THE GOOD PERSON

When I got home from school the next day, I was surprised to see my dad lying on the sofa instead of being away at his office. He worked as a writer for a TV series called *Everyone Loves a Clown*.

"Why aren't you at work?" I asked.

"I—"

"Were you sacked from your job?" I asked.

"No. I—" Dad sneezed and blew his nose into a tissue.

"If you weren't sacked, your series must have been cancelled," I said.

"Shelby, I—"

"It's not your fault that *Everyone Loves a Clown* was cancelled," I said. "That series had the worst title ever. Not everyone loves a clown. Some people think clowns are creepy."

"Listen, Shelby," Dad said. He sneezed again.

"I didn't want to tell you before. But now that your series has been cancelled, I'll be honest," I said. "I think clowns are creepy."

"Shelby," Dad said. "I—"

"With a title like *Everyone Loves a Clown*, I'm surprised that series even got on TV in the first place," I said.

"My series did not get cancelled," Dad said. "I'm at home because I have a bad cold."

"Oh," I said. "In that case, I don't think clowns are

creepy at all. And *Everyone Loves a Clown* is a great title for a series."

Dad sneezed again. He reached into the tissue box.

"Since you're just lying around, you can help me think of ways to be a good person," I said.

"I used up all the tissues in the box," Dad said. "Can you please bring me a new box from the bathroom cupboard?"

I shook my head. "I'm too busy thinking of how to win the Good Person Award."

Lila walked over at that moment. She said, "Shelby, you don't sound like a good person to me."

I scowled at her. "I'm a very good person. But I need to be the best good person in my class."

My mum and my little brother, Coop, came into the room. Mum gave Dad a new box of tissues. Coop gave Dad a broken crayon. Then our dog, Mugsy, bounded into the room. He gave Dad a slobbery lick on his cheek.

"I bet I could win the Good Person Award by ending worldwide hunger," I said.

"That sounds a bit too hard," Dad said.

"How about ending all wars?" I asked.

"Don't be ridiculous, Shelby," my sister said. "How would *you* do something like that?"

"*You* don't be ridiculous, Miss Priss," I told her.

"Shelby," Mum said. "How are you going to end all wars when you can't even stop fighting with your sister?"

"That's right, Shelby," Lila said. "If you really wanted to be a good person, you would clean your side of the bedroom. There's a huge mound of smelly socks by your bed."

"It's not a huge mound of smelly socks. It's just a medium mound," I told Lila. "You always exaggerate, every second of every day."

"I know how you can be the goodest person ever," Coop said. "Buy me a Marvellous Gizmo."

"What is a Marvellous Gizmo?" Dad asked. "I've seen the TV ads and billboards, but I don't really know what it is."

"The coolest toy ever," Cooper, Lila and I said at the same time.

"But what *is* it?" Mum asked.

"It's the toy I'm going to buy with my Good Person Award money," I said. "Now what can I do to win the award?"

"A good person would walk her dog," Mum said.

I shook my head. "That's not good enough to win the award."

"Why don't you pick up litter around the neighbourhood?" Dad suggested.

"I need to do more than that," I said.

"You could help out an elderly person," Mum suggested.

I shook my head again. "Those things aren't good enough to win the award."

Then I had a brilliant idea. I said, "I'll do all three good-person things at once. I'll walk Mugsy, pick up litter along the way and find elderly people to help."

"You'll never be able to do all that," Lila said.

"I certainly will," I said. I grabbed a bin bag, a lead and Mugsy. Then I headed outside. I had an award to win.

A CHAT WITH A COPYCAT

As soon as I left my house, I looked around for elderly people to help. But the only person I saw was Ajay. He wasn't elderly. He was nine. He was dribbling a basketball on his driveway, which was right across the street from my house.

I walked over to Ajay, holding Mugsy's lead in one hand and a large bin bag in my other hand. I asked

64

him, "Do you have any litter around here that needs to be picked up?"

Ajay shook his head.

"Are you sure?" I asked.

"Do you think my family and I are slobs?" Ajay said as he dribbled his ball.

"I don't know if you and your family are slobs. But I want to help out and be a good person," I replied. Then I walked around Ajay's front garden, searching for litter. I couldn't see any.

"Do you want to play basketball?" Ajay called. "It would be nice to have company."

I shook my head. "I can't keep you company. I'm too busy trying to be a good person."

He said, "But—"

"Your basketball looks kind of old," I said. "I'll throw it away for you."

"No!" Ajay clutched the ball against his chest. "Why would you throw out my basketball?"

"I've got a big bin bag to fill," I said.

"Do you want me to help you?" Ajay asked. "We could walk our dogs together and look for litter along the way."

I put my hand on my hip. "Are you trying to steal my idea?"

Ajay glared at me. "First you accuse me of being a litterbug. Then you accuse me of being a thief."

"I never accused you of being a litterbug," I said. "I accused you of being a slob."

"Thanks," Ajay said. He did not sound thankful.

"I also never said you were a thief," I said. "I just think you're a copycat, an imitator, an idea stealer."

"Thanks a lot," Ajay said. He did not sound a lot thankful. He didn't sound even a bit thankful.

"You're welcome." I pointed to his trainers. "Your shoes look old."

"These?" Ajay looked down at his shoes. "I just got these a few weeks ago."

"They didn't last long." I pointed to my bin bag. "Let me throw your trainers away in this very nice, very big, very useful bin bag."

"No!" Ajay said. "Leave my stuff alone."

"I was just trying to help." I shrugged. "Do you know any elderly people around here?"

Ajay glanced around. "Why? Are you going to tell them they're too old and try to put them in your bin bag?"

I laughed.

Ajay did not laugh. He didn't even smile.

"I need to go," I said. "Sorry I can't stay and keep you company."

"I'm not sorry. I've had enough of your company today," Ajay said.

"OK. Have a nice day." I walked away with Mugsy.

A GIGANTIC PROBLEM

I walked around with Mugsy, looking for litter or old people or old people with litter. But my neighbourhood was too clean and too young. Finally, I saw a newspaper lying on a driveway. I picked it up and put it in my bin bag.

A man ran out of the house and down the driveway. He yelled, "Hey, that's my newspaper!"

"You left it lying on the ground," I said. "Luckily, I'm a good person and put it in the rubbish for you."

"You're not a good person. You're a thief!" he yelled. "Give me back my newspaper!"

I handed it to him and sighed. It was hard to be a good person when bad people called me a thief.

"Get away from here," the man said.

"Don't you want me to stay another minute?" I asked.

"No," he said.

I pointed to Mugsy, who was pooing on the man's driveway. Mugsy is a gigantic dog. He makes gigantic poos.

"I mean, yes," the man said. "Stay and clean up your dog's mess."

I did. Then I walked Mugsy for a bit longer. But I didn't see any litter on the ground or elderly people anywhere.

Lucky for me, bin collection was the next day, so rubbish bins lined the street. As we walked by, Mugsy bumped into one of the bins and knocked it over. Rubbish spilled all over the pavement.

Perfect! I started picking up the rubbish and putting it in my bag. When I took my bin bag to school tomorrow, Ms Fish would see for herself that I was a good person who picked up litter. She could also smell that for herself.

I did not like picking up rubbish. It was gross and stinky.

Luckily I saw an elderly woman walking along the street towards me.

I ran over to her, grabbed her arm and said, "I'll help you cross the street." Helping her felt kind of good.

"I'm not going across the street," she said. "Take your hand off my arm. It's dirty and smelly."

"Your arm isn't that dirty or smelly," I said.

"I was talking about your hand," the woman said.

"I Know," I said. "I was joking."

The woman didn't laugh. She didn't even smile.

"Please let me help you," I said. "I want to be a good person and help the elderly."

"Elderly?" the woman asked.

"Yes, elderly," I said. "That means someone who's very old and very wrinkled."

"I'm not elderly," she snapped. "I'm thirty-five years old."

"Oh," I said. "Well, you don't have to be rude. I was trying to be a good person."

The not-elderly woman frowned at me. "A good person does not insult a young woman by calling her elderly."

Mugsy pulled hard on his lead and got away from me. He knocked the bin bag out of my hands. He knocked the not-elderly woman onto her bottom. Then he ran down the street.

"Help me up," the not-elderly woman said. "Give me a hand."

"I can't. My hand is dirty and smelly, remember?" I said. "And you're not elderly. So helping you wouldn't count much for the Good Person Award. Plus I have to get Mugsy."

I raced after him.

FOLLOW THAT DOG

As I raced away, the not-elderly woman yelled, "Your bag of rubbish is all over my lawn!"

"I'll come back," I yelled, "because I'm a good person!"

"No you're not!" she yelled back.

I kept running.

Mugsy stopped half a street ahead of me, in front of a small flower garden. Phew! I ran over. Before I could

reach him, Mugsy weed on the flower garden and hurried off. I followed him.

Ahead of us was a woman who looked about a thousand years old. She was walking slowly with a cane. What bad luck! I'd finally found a truly elderly person to help, but I was too busy chasing after my dog.

Mugsy ran right towards the truly elderly person.

"Mugsy! Stop!" I yelled.

Fortunately Mugsy swerved out of the truly elderly woman's way just in time.

Unfortunately the truly elderly woman jabbed Mugsy with her cane. She yelled, "Scram, wild beast! Scram!"

"That's no wild beast," I said. "That's my dog."

"Well, your dog is acting like a wild beast. And you let him run loose," she said. "I'm going to report you to the authorities. What's your name?"

"Go ahead and report me. My name is Brooke Crumpkin," I said.

"Shelby!" Ajay said, running towards me. "Do you need help?"

"Who is Shelby?" the truly elderly woman asked. "You said your name was Brooke Crumpkin."

I didn't respond to her. I hurried after Mugsy.

"Ajay, please help me get Mugsy!" I yelled over my shoulder.

Mugsy ran through the neighbourhood, wagging his tail the whole time. He weed on a patch of grass. He weed on the pavement. He weed on a lamp post. He weed on a sign that said, "No dogs allowed."

Ajay and I got close to Mugsy a few times, but he kept racing away. Finally, after Ajay and I could hardly breathe or move, Mugsy ran home.

Standing on the front porch, Mum said, "You were gone a long time. I was worried about you. Why aren't you holding Mugsy's lead?"

"Need" — I panted — "water."

"Need" – Ajay panted – "to" – he panted – "sit" – he panted – "down" – he panted.

We all went into the house. Ajay, Mugsy and I drank a lot of water. Then Ajay and I flopped onto the living room sofa. Mugsy ran around inside the house.

My sister walked into the living room, stared at Ajay and me and said, "You two look awful."

I frowned at her and said, "Thanks a lot."

She smiled at me and replied, "You're welcome."

My brother, Coop, ran in, spun around in circles, did a somersault and then jumped on the sofa next to me.

"Mum, do something," I complained.

"I *am* doing something," she said. "I'm filming you kids for my blog."

She filmed Ajay and me slumped on the sofa. She filmed Coop jumping up and down next to us. Then she said, "What happened today on your walk?"

I told Mum about:

1. The angry, not-elderly woman
2. The angry man with the newspaper
3. Mugsy's escape
4. The spilled bag of rubbish
5. The angry, truly elderly woman

After I finished talking, Lila said, "You made a lot of people angry. You don't sound like a good person to me."

Mum said, "You need to pick up that rubbish."

I said, "I can't. I'm too tired."

"You can and you will," Mum said. "I'll drive you to the house where you spilled the rubbish."

"I'll help you, Shelby," Ajay said.

"Me too!" cried Coop. "Rubbish! Yay! Fun!"

I sighed. I did not think rubbish was either *yay* or *fun*. Mugsy jumped on the sofa and wagged his tail.

"Sorry, Mugsy. You're staying at home. You have had enough adventure today," Mum said. "But, Lila, you're coming with us to help."

Lila sighed too and said, "I don't want to help."

"You don't sound like a good person to me," I told her.

Mum drove us to the area where the rubbish had spilled from my bag. We got out of the car, put on rubber gloves and started picking up rubbish. It felt kind of good to clean up.

Just then the not-elderly woman walked over to us. She said, "Brooke Crumpkin, I was just about to report you to the authorities for littering."

"Who?" Mum asked.

"The authorities," the not-elderly woman said.

"I meant who is Brooke Crumpkin?" Mum said.

The not-elderly woman pointed to me. "I overheard her say her name was Brooke Crumpkin."

Mum raised her eyebrows at me.

"Her name is Shelby Bloom," Lila said.

"I'm sorry," I said as I picked up more rubbish. "I'm really, really sorry. I try to be a good person, but I keep making things worse. I promise I'll clean everything up."

I would never get the Good Person Award at this rate. I just hoped I wouldn't get the Bad Person Award, which they'd have to invent just for me.

MORE THAN ONE LAUGHING STOCK

The next morning, my family ate yummy pancakes together at the kitchen table.

Mum said, "Yesterday my blog got the most hits ever! Some people said my post was the funniest thing they'd ever read."

"Wuh wry bout?" I asked.

"What?" Mum asked.

"Shelby, it's rude to talk with your mouth full," Miss Priss said.

I swallowed my pancakes and said, "What did you write about?"

"I wrote about your day yesterday," Mum said. "I wrote that you called a young woman elderly, tried to throw away an unread newspaper and had to chase Mugsy around the neighbourhood."

I glared at her. "You wrote about all my mistakes on your blog?"

"I didn't just *write* about your mistakes," Mum said. "I also posted a picture of you slumped on the sofa, looking completely worn out. And I posted a video of you picking up the spilled rubbish."

"Rubbish! Yay!" Coop said.

Lila laughed.

"Lila, you were in the video too," Mum said.

Lila stopped laughing.

Mum said, "My readers thought it was so funny when you picked up one piece of rubbish, said I was torturing you, and then sat in the car while everyone else cleaned up the rest."

"Rubbish! Yay!" Coop repeated.

"Picking up that piece of rubbish was one of the worst moments of my life," Lila said.

"Rubbish! Yay!" Coop said again.

"Lila, you don't sound like a good person to me," I said.

"Being a good person doesn't have to be hard," Dad said. "You can be a good person by doing something simple."

I shook my head and said, "Last time you suggested something simple, I became a laughing stock on Mum's blog."

"You aren't a laughing stock," Mum said. "My readers just think you're funny."

That sounded like the same thing to me.

"Shelby, yesterday we suggested a few simple acts of kindness," Dad said. "But you tried to do three of them at once – walking Mugsy, picking up litter and helping the elderly."

"Litter! Yay!" Coop said.

"Why don't you try just doing one simple, nice thing this morning?" Dad said. "For instance, you could offer to carry someone's schoolbooks."

"OK." I picked up Lila's history book.

"Your hands are full of syrup!" Lila grabbed her book. "Ugh. Now my book is all sticky. You don't sound like a good person to me."

"Girls, be nice," Dad said.

"OK, let's hug," I said. I hugged Lila, clasping my sticky hands around her arms.

"You just got syrup on my arms," Lila said.

I held back a laugh.

"Can I hug you?" Coop asked Lila. "I don't have syrup on my hands."

"Sure," she said.

He hugged her.

Lila stepped back and said, "You have *something* on your hands."

Coop shrugged. "Just a little drool."

I laughed while Lila ran to the bathroom to wash her arms.

GOOD PERSON OR BIG, SCARY GIRL?

I spent the whole trip to school thinking about how to be a good person. I thought about it as I walked to the school bus, as I waited for the school bus and as I sat on the school bus.

I couldn't come up with anything. So I decided to use Dad's idea to carry someone's schoolbooks. But I didn't see anyone holding books. Most kids kept their books in their backpacks.

I paced outside the school and watched people arrive. Luckily, I finally saw a person holding a book in her arms. *Un*luckily, that person was Brooke.

I hurried over to her and said, "Let me carry that book for you."

"No way! You just want to act like a good person," Brooke said. "I'll carry *your* book."

"No way!" I said.

Brooke lunged forward and grabbed onto my book with one hand. I lunged forward and grabbed onto her book with one hand. Brooke clung to her book with her other hand. I clung to my book with my other hand.

We stood in front of the school, lunging and yanking on each other's books like we were playing a game of book tug-of-war. Book tug-of-war was not a fun game. In fact, it was an awful game. Book tug-of-war was the worst game I'd ever played.

As I pulled on my book, I felt something soft behind me. I looked at the soft thing. It was a little girl. She stumbled.

Then Brooke bumped into her and knocked her over. The little girl fell onto the pavement on her bottom.

"You big, mean bullies!" the little girl said.

"I'm sorry," I told her.

Brooke pointed to the little girl and said, "You shouldn't have got in our way."

I reached out my hand to help the little girl. As I did, Brooke grabbed my book.

"Ha!" she said. "I will carry your book to class and win the Good Person Award!" She quickly walked away.

I gently lifted the little girl up and said, "I'm sorry" again. She scrunched her little nose as if she was about to cry.

Oh no. I needed to cheer her up. I said. "How about a joke? What do you call a bear with no teeth?"

The little girl shrugged.

"A gummy bear," I said.

The little girl frowned.

"Don't worry. The dentist gave the bear new teeth," I said. "Guess what was the first thing the bear ate?"

The little girl did not guess.

"The dentist." I laughed.

The little girl kept frowning.

Gabby walked over. She crouched in front of the little girl and said, "Are you OK?"

"No," the little girl said. She pointed at me. "That big, scary girl knocked me down."

"She's big, but I don't think she's scary," Gabby said. "Not *that* scary anyway. Do you want an invisible, magic bandage?"

The little girl nodded.

Gabby pretended to take something out of her pocket. Then she pretended to put it on the girl's forehead. "This invisible, magic bandage will make you feel better right away," she said.

The little girl smiled. "Thank you! Now I feel better."

She gave Gabby a hug. She gave me a frown. I didn't want her to be scared of me. Just then the bell rang.

"How did the ocean say goodbye?" I asked.

The little girl shrugged.

"It waved."

The little girl finally laughed. It felt kind of good to cheer her up. Gabby and I waved goodbye to the little girl and walked to our classroom.

On the way in, I told Gabby, "All my plans to be a good person keep failing. I need a lot more time if I'm going to win the award."

As we entered the classroom, I froze. In big letters on the whiteboard Ms Fish had written, "The Good Person Award will be given today."

THE WINNER IS...

As I sat at my desk, I had a lump in my throat. Ms Fish was going to name the winner of the Good Person Award, and that name wasn't going to be Shelby Bloom. I had tried so hard, but I had failed at everything I'd done.

I remembered everything that went wrong:

1. I'd made brownies. But I'd also made a big mess

in my kitchen, made two of my classmates throw up and made ants invade my classroom.

2. I had tried to help out at the school library. But I'd messed up the school library.

3. I had tried to walk my dog, pick up litter and help the elderly. But I'd lost my dog, knocked over a rubbish bin and annoyed the elderly and not elderly.

4. I had tried to carry people's books. But Lila had got syrup and drool on her, and a little girl had tripped over Brooke and me.

Basically I had the worst chance of anyone in my class at winning the award.

"I know I'm going to win," Brooke said loudly.

Never mind. Brooke Crumpkin had the worst chance at winning the award.

Ms Fish said she would wait until everyone was quiet and sitting in their seats. Everyone rushed to their seats and stopped talking.

Then Ms Fish made a speech about how we'd all learned something about being good for the sake of being good. I wasn't sure what that meant. So maybe I hadn't learned something about being good or goodness sakes or whatever Ms Fish said we'd learned. The most important thing was that Ms Fish was finally going to announce the winner.

"The winner of the Good Person Award is a very good person," Ms Fish announced. "The winner is Gabby Garcia."

The class clapped and cheered. I was happy for Gabby. She really was a good person.

"Gabby is well-behaved in class," Ms Fish said. "She puts her hand up before talking."

Brooke shouted. "Not fair!"

Ms Fish ignored Brooke. "Gabby never interrupts people when—"

"I deserve that award," Brooke interrupted.

"—they're speaking. Gabby is modest," the teacher said.

"I'm the very best person in this class or any other class," Brooke said.

"Gabby is kind to others," Ms Fish said.

"Everyone here stinks," Brooke said. "I want that award."

"Brooke Crumpkin, I'm about to award you with a trip to the head teacher's office," Ms Fish said.

Brooke finally stopped talking.

Gabby deserved the award. She picked up litter from the school playground. She shelved books in the school library. She brought in cupcakes that were allergy-free, gluten-free and vegan. And somehow they'd still tasted good. She had cleaned up the brownie and cake crumbs. She had cheered up a little girl this morning. She probably did a lot more good stuff that I didn't even know about. Plus she was a nice friend.

"Congratulations, Gabby," I said. I started clapping.

Almost everyone else clapped too. Gabby didn't clap, because she was modest. Brooke didn't clap, because she was selfish. Jack Lopez didn't clap, because he was texting on his mobile phone.

After we'd finished clapping, Ms Fish took Jack's mobile phone away. Then she said, "There is one more winner of the Good Person Award. . . ."

A GREAT SURPRISE AND A TERRIBLE SURPRISE

Brooke pulled back her chair and stood up. She said, "Ms Fish, I knew you would give me the Good Person Award. Gabby's a pretty good person, but I am the *best* good person."

"Sit down, Brooke," Ms Fish said. "You did not win the award. The other winner of the Good Person Award is Shelby Bloom."

My mouth dropped open in surprise. I closed it and said, "Me?"

Brooke sneered and said, "Her?"

"Yes," Ms Fish said. "Shelby has tried very hard to be a good person. After she made brownies for the class, she had to clean up a huge mess in her kitchen."

"How do you know about that?" I asked.

"I read your mother's blog," Ms Fish said.

My mouth dropped open again. I remembered all the embarrassing things my mum had put on her blog. Then I realized something else – the blog had helped me win the Good Person Award. I closed my mouth and smiled.

"I also talked to the school librarian," Ms Fish said.

I cringed.

"If you talked to the librarian, why are you giving me the award?" I asked Ms Fish.

"She told me you brought a lot of lonely kids together," Ms Fish said. "Those kids had been sitting by themselves in the library every day. They came together to help you put books away. They laughed at your jokes and became friends."

"They did?" I asked. I had no idea. Maybe it was lucky I had knocked over the books.

"Shelby also walked her dog, picked up litter and tried to help a woman she thought was elderly," Ms Fish said. "Her plans didn't always work."

"Shelby's plans *never* work," Brooke said.

"Shelby's plans to be a good person didn't work out the way she thought they would," Ms Fish said. "But she brought laughter to a lot of people – including me."

"Shelby almost made a little girl cry this morning," Brooke said with a sneer.

"Shelby also made a little girl laugh this morning," Gabby said with a smile.

"Gabby and Shelby, come up and get your Good Person Awards," Ms Fish said.

This was the big moment! I couldn't wait to get my money or gift certificate. I'd go to the shops after school and buy the coolest thing ever – a Marvellous Gizmo.

I hurried to the front of the classroom. Along the way, I accidentally stepped on Latasha Kennedy's toe, knocked a stack of papers off Will Carelli's desk and jabbed my elbow into Jack Lopez's ear. I hoped Ms Fish wouldn't change her mind about giving me the Good Person Award.

I got to the front of the classroom and waited for Gabby. She was picking up the papers I'd knocked off Will's desk. Finally, Gabby finished and stood next to me.

Ms Fish handed each of us a rolled-up piece of paper. I unrolled my paper slowly. I thought, *It must be a gift certificate!* I hoped it was for a lot of money. Marvellous Gizmos were expensive.

But the paper wasn't a gift certificate. It was just a piece of paper that said *Shelby Bloom Is the Winner of the Good Person Award in Ms Fish's Class.*

Next to me, Gabby said, "Thank you! I'm so happy!"

I looked at Gabby's paper. It looked just like mine, except with Gabby's name on it.

"Do we get any money or a gift certificate?" I asked.

Ms Fish shook her head.

"I don't need money or a gift certificate," Gabby said. "I like helping others and being a good person. It feels good to be honoured for my service."

I rolled my eyes.

If I weren't such a good person, I would have told Gabby to be quiet.

EVEN BETTER THAN A MARVELLOUS GIZMO

"What's wrong?" Mum asked me when I got home from school.

"How do you know something's wrong?" I asked.

"You're frowning, your arms are crossed and you're stomping around the house," she said.

"I'll tell you what's wrong." I threw my backpack on the floor and flopped down on the living room sofa. "I won the Good Person Award."

"How wonderful!" Mum said. "You worked so hard for that award."

"Wrong," I said. "I mean, you're right about me working hard for the award. But the award isn't wonderful. All I got was this." I unzipped my backpack, reached between my maths textbook and my leftover lunch, and pulled out my Good Person Award. The paper was wrinkled and smelled like tuna.

Mum took the award from me. She grinned as if she were looking at a thousand-dollar bill. "How wonderful!" she said again.

"But I didn't get any money with the award," I said. "I wanted to buy a Marvellous Gizmo."

"I'm so proud of you, Shelby," Mum said. "I'll buy you a Marvellous Gizmo for winning the award."

"Now that's wonderful!" I exclaimed.

"What is a Marvellous Gizmo anyway?" Mum asked.

"The coolest thing ever," I said. "Let's go to the shops now."

"After dinner," Mum said.

"*Mu-u-um,*" I whined. Then I reminded myself I was a good person. I also reminded myself that Mum could still change her mind about buying me a Marvellous Gizmo. So I stopped whining.

I helped Mum and Dad make dinner and clean up afterwards so we could leave for the shops faster. It felt kind of good to help out. Finally Mum drove me to the shops. Along the way, we heard two radio ads and saw two billboards for Marvellous Gizmos.

I said, "These ads say Marvellous Gizmos are the coolest toys ever."

Mum glanced at me and said, "If Marvellous Gizmos really were the coolest toys ever, they wouldn't need so much advertising."

I thought about that. Mum might have a point.

As soon as Mum parked in the car park, I hurried out of the car. Brooke got out of a car nearby.

"What are *you* doing here, Shelby?" she said.

"Buying a Marvellous Gizmo," I said as I hurried towards the shop. "What are you doing here?"

"Seeing if I can return my Marvellous Gizmo," Brooke said. "I was upset about not winning the Good Person Award, so my parents bought me a Marvellous Gizmo to cheer me up. But I want to return it for something better."

"You want to return the coolest toy ever?" I asked.

"I thought the Marvellous Gizmo would be the coolest toy ever," Brooke said as we walked. "But it's not cool at all. It's small, and it doesn't do much. It's the most boring toy ever."

"Oh," I said.

I started walking more slowly. Brooke rushed past me and into the shop.

Mum caught up with me at the entrance to the toy shop. Her friend Ms Cho was outside the shop. She was collecting donations.

"I'm collecting money for sick and injured kids in the hospital," she told us.

I thought of the Marvellous Gizmos inside the toy shop. I thought about what my mum had said about them on the way here. I thought about what Brooke had just said about them. I thought about sick and injured children in hospital.

I told my mum, "Instead of buying me a Marvellous Gizmo, will you donate to the children in the hospital?"

"How wonderful!" Mum said again. "You're such a good person!"

It felt good to help sick and injured kids. Of course, it would also feel good to buy new toys. So I told Mum, "Please hurry up and donate the money before I change my mind."

"All right." Mum hugged me and said, "Now I'm more proud of you than ever."

I smiled. It felt good to be a good person.

D.L. Green has written **32** books for children and teens, including the Zeke Meeks and Silver Pony Ranch humorous chapter book series. Her books have been translated into six other languages. She lives in California, USA, and has a nice husband, three great kids and a spoiled dog. As well as writing funny books, she works as a lawyer.

Illustrator Leandra La Rosa lives and works in Palermo, Sicily. She was born in Trapani, a town on the island's western side, and since childhood her main interests have been illustration, animation and music. Leandra studied at the Academy of Fine Arts in Palermo and obtained a degree in graphic design. Since 2013 she has been working as a graphic designer and illustrator for many Italian agencies and publishing houses.

READ THEM ALL!